THE VOICE OF THE POET

Series Editor: J.D. McClatchy

John Ashbery

Random House AudioBooks

NEW YORK, NEW YORK

CONTENTS

In certain poems the audio version differs from the published text.

JOHN ASHBERY

In his prose poem "The New Spirit," John Ashbery poses the interesting dilemma at the heart of his work: "I thought I could put it all down, that would be one way. And next the thought came to me that to leave it all out would be another, and truer, way." All along, there have been readers of Ashbery's work who thought that everything they'd been accustomed to find in a poem—from music to meaning—had been *left out*. They were first bored or baffled and, when Ashbery's poetry eventually moved from the avant-garde fringe to the critical spotlight, they were outraged. For his admirers, on the other hand, what Ashbery had left out were all the tired conventions, the dull patter, the highfalutin metaphors, the sour confessions of the kind of mid-century poetries that had dominated before his mysterious, campy, disjunctive note sounded. And for Ashbery himself, a quarter century ago, much the same thing happened. He had been publishing books that were read by few and ignored by most. Then suddenly in 1975, he published his fifth collection, *Self-Portrait in a Convex Mirror*. Not only was critical attention lavished on the book, but the poet was given that year's Pulitzer Prize, National Book Award, and National Book Critics Circle Award—an unprecedented hat trick. The only trouble was that he had passed from obscurity to celebrity without any intervening period of being understood. The poet was bemused. His admirers felt vindicated without knowing why. His detractors sniffed but felt uneasy.

Gertrude Stein said that, in order to read literature properly, we ought to begin at the beginning. And the beginning, she added, is now. Few contemporary poets have seemed so to be starting *now* as Ashbery. But that starting-point can be viewed from two perspectives. First, his work derives from some of the peculiar strands of thought and art in the twentieth century. French existentialism, for instance, with its emphasis on the "actual" over the "real," on the sense that constant change alone is freedom. And later, French theories of deconstruction, with their emphasis on the absence of the Author, the sense that a text assembles itself through a writer but not because of him. Or take the painters who as a group are known now as the abstract expressionists or "action" painters. For them, a painting was a process, not a product; their subject was the making of the picture itself. Ashbery's long residence in Paris and his fascination with French writing, his intimate friendships with the painters of the New York School—there is every reason to suppose he caught "the new spirit" in the air. But there is another sense of *now* at work in Ashbery's poems, one that refers not to the age but to the moment. As one poem puts it:

> For although memories, of a season, for
>   example,
> Melt into a single snapshot, one cannot
>   guard, treasure
> That stalled moment. It too is flowing,
>   fleeting!

The aesthetic strain in twentieth-century poetry derives from Walter Pater's notion of "the privileged moment" when all revolves around a still point lit by his hard gem-like flame. Ashbery knows better. In the blur of modern urban life, in the glut of images and information that engulfs our daily lives, it is impossible to pretend there is a "stalled moment." So, rather than use language to construct stationary but illusory perspectives, he uses the poem as a kind of continuum, a solution in which events and ideas and feeling float freely. The effect is rather like overhearing a radio in the next room whose dial someone is slowly turning: one minute Beethoven, the next hip-hop, the next a traffic report. All is equal in the "flowing, fleeting" moment, nothing is excluded or judged. Ashbery has made consciousness itself into art. As far back as 1961, he was quoting with approval a statement by the French artist and writer Henri Michaux, one that summarizes Ashbery's own ambitions from the start:

> Instead of one vision which excludes others, I would have liked to draw the moments that, placed side by side, go to make up a life. To expose the interior phrase for people to see, the phrase that has no words, a rope which sinuously and intimately accompanies everything that impinges from the outside or inside. I wanted to draw the consciousness of existence and the flow of time. As you would take your pulse.

His desire, as he has told interviewers, is "to pick up whatever is in the air . . . the disparate circumstances that as I say are with us at every moment . . . to reproduce the polyphony that goes on inside me, which I don't think is radically different from that of other people." The reader then is "somehow given an embodiment out of those proliferating reflections that are occurring in a generalized mind which eventually run together into the image of a specific person, 'he' or 'me' who was not there when the poem began." It is an enterprise that risks the trivial and boring and confusing, and that seems to threaten our received ideas of poetry. But Ashbery has triumphed over such doubts and produced, in book after book, an astonishing portrait of The Way We Live Now. It's a portrait that is funny and tender. If you're listening properly, you will indeed hear your own pulse.

For all of his cosmopolitan ways, John Ashbery was born in the country. His father was a fruit farmer in Sodus, New York, a small town near Lake Ontario. His mother Helen has been a high-school biology teacher, and her own father—in whose library the young Ashbery read voraciously—was a physicist teaching at the University of Rochester. Ashbery,

In Acapulco, 1955

who was born in 1927, also had a younger brother who died of leukemia at age nine. Loneliness became a condition. He was sent away to boarding school at Deerfield, and then enrolled at Harvard in 1945. It was his seedbed. His studies flourished, as did his friendships with such classmates as Frank O'Hara and Kenneth Koch, and his literary ambitions (he worked on the *Harvard Advocate*) began to take shape. After graduation, he moved to New York to study French literature at Columbia, and received his M.A. two years later. But New York City had more to teach him than Columbia, and Ashbery fell in with a remarkable group of writers and painters (among them James Schuyler, Fairfield Porter, Larry Rivers, and Jane Freilicher) whose work shared the same energies. When he had finally assembled a suitable manuscript, he submitted it to the Yale Young Poets competition, as did Frank O'Hara. The judge was W. H. Auden. The story goes that Auden, dissatisfied with the manuscripts the Press had sent him that year, asked to see the work by two poets he'd heard of and knew had submitted but been screened out early, O'Hara and Ashbery. He chose Ashbery, and *Some Trees* was published in 1956. (Later in his life, Auden told a friend he hadn't understood a word Ashbery had written.) Influenced by the obliquities of Wallace Stevens and Auden himself, it was an austere beginning, but one poem in the book, "The Instruction Manual," with its daydreaming leaps of language, pointed ahead to his more mature work.

In 1955 he received a Fulbright Fellowship and

moved to Paris for two years, then returned in 1958 and stayed for a decade, writing for the *New York Herald Tribune* and *ArtNews* to support himself. One result of those years was his second book, *The Tennis Court Oath,* his most forbidding collection. It is a heap of cut-out fragments glued haphazardly together. Even those who admired his radical experimentation considered it a dead end. Ashbery himself once said that he was "taking poetry apart to try to understand how it works." Putting it back together again was the job of *Rivers and Mountains* (1966), *The Double Dream of Spring* (1970), and *Three Poems* (1972). By this time he had, after the death of his father, returned to New York and started working as an editor and journalist. His poems grow more lyrical, more eloquent, more substantial. One begins now to hear the plangency that marks all his subsequent work, the collisions and fresh starts out of which he makes poetry:

> The extreme austerity of an almost
>   empty mind
> Colliding with the lush, Rousseau-like
>   foliage of its desire to communicate
> Something between breaths, if only for
>   the sake
> Of others and their desire to understand
>   you and desert you
> For other centers of communication, so
>   that understanding
> May begin, and in doing so be undone.

The dazzling success of *Self-Portrait in a Convex Mirror* and of *Houseboat Days* (1977) may owe something to the fact that by then Ashbery had not only abandoned his early experimental style and embraced a peculiar kind of post-modern Romanticism but had engaged more directly some of poetry's most familiar themes—the fragility of the self, the wages of mortality, the passage of time, the contingencies of art. What Wallace Stevens called the "mind in the act of finding" moves in these poems through spaces at once more intimate and more accessible (including the studio of the sixteenth-century Italian Mannerist painter Parmigianino).

In the 60s he was writing plays and, in collaboration with James Schuyler, a novel. Ashbery consistently pushed his talent in new directions. His next book of poems, *As We Know* (1979), was written on two sides of a notebook, on different days, and published as a poem in two columns meant to be read simultaneously. But as before, the impulse toward extremes was followed by a retreat—and a strengthening. *A Wave* (1984) is one of Ashbery's best books, and its title poem broods on love and death in ways that may have been prompted by the serious spinal infection that nearly killed him in 1982. A MacArthur Award in 1985 allowed him to resign as *Newsweek*'s art critic, though since 1974 he has continued to teach, first at Brooklyn College and now at Bard. New books appear, as regular as clockwork: *April Galleons* (1987), *Flow Chart* (1991), *Hotel Lautréamont* (1992), *And the Stars Were Shining* (1994), *Can You Hear*

Me, Bird (1995), *Girls on the Run* (1999), and *Your Name Here* (2000). A collection of his art criticism, *Reported Sightings,* appeared in 1989, and his Harvard lectures on minor poets, *Other Traditions,* were published in 2000.

John Ashbery has always been a figure out of the recent future, unpredictable and innovative. Like his earliest influence, Auden, he has rigorously explored the byways of formal possibilities in verse, and looked under more rocks of contemporary life than most any other poet of his generation, continually discovering freshened channels of poetic energy. The even, uninflected tone of the poet's reading voice (a manner he shares with one of his idols, Elizabeth Bishop) may at times hide the remarkable range of idiom and tone in his work, as he offers us what he calls his "paradigms of common experience"—or better, the experience of experience. "I look out my window," he says of living in New York City, "and see what seems to be a Gothic church tower and a big building that says ABIE's BABY on it right next door." But his voice is low-key as if to accommodate both the high rhetoric of traditional verse *and* the clichés and banalities of everyday speech. The result is, in his own words, "a kind of confused but insistent impression of the culture going on around us." "I write with experiences in mind," he adds, "but I don't write about them, I write out of them." William James once said that truth *happens* to an idea, and in much the same way meanings *happen* to an

Ashbery poem. Different readers at different times in different ways will read into these poems what they find there—their own ways of thinking reflected back at them.

"Very often people don't listen to you when you speak to them," he's wryly noted. "It's only when you talk to yourself that they prick up their ears." And in an important sense, Ashbery is talking to himself, while noise goes on around him. He has said that what he listens to is another self; that he thinks of himself as *John,* and of the person who writes his poems as *Ashbery.* To understand his poems, it's crucial to listen to the continual dialogue between *John* and *Ashbery.* Their back-and-forth gives shape and momentum to a poem, and when they are braided and streaming across the mind's ear the results can be very heady indeed. One of his poems speaks of "trees / Of two minds half-caught in their buzz and luster." Those are the two tones, the two voices in dialogue: buzz and luster. *Buzz* is the clutter around him: bits of opera and old movies, gossip and newspaper articles and Greek tragedy, the dog chasing its tail on the living-room rug. It's the voice of *John,* and it can be abstract and colloquial, rational or journalistic, witty or silly. *Luster* is the deep call of memory, desire, impulse, art. It is *Ashbery,* and can sound romantic, fantastic, sublime. It is the voice of the imagination, counter-pointed with and surging up through the noise of life. The drama in these poems is all about "holding on to the hard earth so as not to get thrown off, / With an occasional dream, a vision." Each poem, in other words, is a little stage on which are enacted the terms of our lives, what-we-have and what-we-want always at odds. Ashbery's poems reach for themselves and for their readers "through vagrant sympathy and a kind of immediate contact." They wander back to their sources of power, then sidle up to us. We recognize their accents as our own, but hear too the way speech yearns towards the vision within. We are hearing the echoes of dreams inside the narrow prison cell of the individual mind. We are watching the strange weaving and unweaving of ourselves.

J. D. McClatchy

Soonest Mended

Barely tolerated, living on the margin
In our technological society, we were always having to be
    rescued
On the brink of destruction, like heroines in *Orlando Furioso*
Before it was time to start all over again.
There would be thunder in the bushes, a rustling of coils,
And Angelica, in the Ingres painting, was considering
The colorful but small monster near her toe, as though
    wondering whether forgetting
The whole thing might not, in the end, be the only
    solution.
And then there always came a time when
Happy Hooligan in his rusted green automobile
Came plowing down the course, just to make sure
    everything was O.K.,
Only by that time we were in another chapter and confused
About how to receive this latest piece of information.
Was it information? Weren't we rather acting this out
For someone else's benefit, thoughts in a mind
With room enough and to spare for our little problems (so
    they began to seem),
Our daily quandary about food and the rent and bills to be
    paid?
To reduce all this to a small variant,
To step free at last, minuscule on the gigantic plateau—
This was our ambition: to be small and clear and free.
Alas, the summer's energy wanes quickly,
A moment and it is gone. And no longer
May we make the necessary arrangements, simple as they are.
Our star was brighter perhaps when it had water in it.
Now there is no question even of that, but only
Of holding on to the hard earth so as not to get thrown off,

With an occasional dream, a vision: a robin flies across
The upper corner of the window, you brush your hair away
And cannot quite see, or a wound will flash
Against the sweet faces of the others, something like:
This is what you wanted to hear, so why
Did you think of listening to something else? We are all
    talkers
It is true, but underneath the talk lies
The moving and not wanting to be moved, the loose
Meaning, untidy and simple like a threshing floor.

These then were some hazards of the course,
Yet though we knew the course *was* hazards and nothing else
It was still a shock when, almost a quarter of a century later,
The clarity of the rules dawned on you for the first time.
They were the players, and we who had struggled at the game
Were merely spectators, though subject to its vicissitudes
And moving with it out of the tearful stadium, borne on
    shoulders, at last.
Night after night this message returns, repeated
In the flickering bulbs of the sky, raised past us, taken away
    from us,
Yet ours over and over until the end that is past truth,
The being of our sentences, in the climate that fostered them,
Not ours to own, like a book, but to be with, and sometimes
To be without, alone and desperate.
But the fantasy makes it ours, a kind of fence-sitting
Raised to the level of an esthetic ideal. These were moments,
    years,
Solid with reality, faces, namable events, kisses, heroic acts,
But like the friendly beginning of a geometrical progression

Not too reassuring, as though meaning could be cast aside some day
    some day
When it had been outgrown. Better, you said, to stay cowering
    cowering
Like this in the early lessons, since the promise of learning
Is a delusion, and I agreed, adding that
Tomorrow would alter the sense of what had already been learned,
    learned,
That the learning process is extended in this way, so that from this standpoint
    from this standpoint
None of us ever graduates from college,
For time is an emulsion, and probably thinking not to grow up
    grow up
Is the brightest kind of maturity for us, right now at any rate.
    rate.
And you see, both of us were right, though nothing
Has somehow come to nothing; the avatars
Of our conforming to the rules and living
Around the home have made—well, in a sense, "good citizens" of us,
    citizens" of us,
Brushing the teeth and all that, and learning to accept
The charity of the hard moments as they are doled out,
For this is action, this not being sure, this careless
Preparing, sowing the seeds crooked in the furrow,
Making ready to forget, and always coming back
To the mooring of starting out, that day so long ago.

1970

Parergon

We are happy in our way of life.
It doesn't make much sense to others. We sit about,
Read, and are restless. Occasionally it becomes time
To lower the dark shade over it all.
Our entity pivots on a self-induced trance
Like sleep. Noiseless our living stops
And one strays as in a dream
Into those respectable purlieus where life is motionless and
    alive
To utter the few words one knows:

"O woebegone people! Why so much crying,
Such desolation in the streets?
Is it the present of flesh, that each of you
At your jagged casement window should handle,
Nervous unto thirst and ultimate death?
Meanwhile the true way is sleeping;
Your lawful acts drink an unhealthy repose
From the upturned lip of this vessel, secretly,
But it is always time for a change.
That certain sins of omission go unpunished
Does not weaken your position
But this underbrush in which you are secure
Is its doing. Farewell then,
Until, under a better sky
We may meet expended, for just doing it
Is only an excuse. We need the tether
Of entering each other's lives, eyes wide apart, crying."

As one who moves forward from a dream
The stranger left that house on hastening feet
Leaving behind the woman with the face shaped like an
  arrowhead,
And all who gazed upon him wondered at
The strange activity around him.
How fast the faces kindled as he passed!
It was a marvel that no one spoke
To stem the river of his passing
Now grown to flood proportions, as on the sunlit mall
Or in the enclosure of some court
He took his pleasure, savage
And mild with the contemplating.
Yet each knew he saw only aspects,
That the continuity was fierce beyond all dream of
  enduring,
And turned his head away, and so
The lesson eddied far into the night:
Joyful its beams, and in the blackness blacker still,
Though undying joyousness, caught in that trap.

1970

I don't think my poetry is inaccessible. People
say it's very private, but I think it's about the
privacy of everyone.

Self-Portrait in a Convex Mirror

As Parmigianino did it, the right hand
Bigger than the head, thrust at the viewer
And swerving easily away, as though to protect
What it advertises. A few leaded panes, old beams,
Fur, pleated muslin, a coral ring run together
In a movement supporting the face, which swims
Toward and away like the hand
Except that it is in repose. It is what is
Sequestered. Vasari says, "Francesco one day set himself
To take his own portrait, looking at himself for that
     purpose
In a convex mirror, such as is used by barbers . . .
He accordingly caused a ball of wood to be made
By a turner, and having divided it in half and
Brought it to the size of the mirror, he set himself
With great art to copy all that he saw in the glass,"
Chiefly his reflection, of which the portrait
Is the reflection once removed.
The glass chose to reflect only what he saw
Which was enough for his purpose: his image
Glazed, embalmed, projected at a 180-degree angle.
The time of day or the density of the light
Adhering to the face keeps it
Lively and intact in a recurring wave
Of arrival. The soul establishes itself.
But how far can it swim out through the eyes
And still return safely to its nest? The surface
Of the mirror being convex, the distance increases
Significantly; that is, enough to make the point
That the soul is a captive, treated humanely, kept
In suspension, unable to advance much farther
Than your look as it intercepts the picture.

Pope Clement and his court were "stupefied"
By it, according to Vasari, and promised a commission
That never materialized. The soul has to stay where it is,
Even though restless, hearing raindrops at the pane,
The sighing of autumn leaves thrashed by the wind,
Longing to be free, outside, but it must stay
Posing in this place. It must move
As little as possible. This is what the portrait says.
But there is in that gaze a combination
Of tenderness, amusement and regret, so powerful
In its restraint that one cannot look for long.
The secret is too plain. The pity of it smarts,
Makes hot tears spurt: that the soul is not a soul,
Has no secret, is small, and it fits
Its hollow perfectly: its room, our moment of attention.
That is the tune but there are no words.
The words are only speculation
(From the Latin *speculum,* mirror):
They seek and cannot find the meaning of the music.
We see only postures of the dream,
Riders of the motion that swings the face
Into view under evening skies, with no
False disarray as proof of authenticity.
But it is life englobed.
One would like to stick one's hand
Out of the globe, but its dimension,
What carries it, will not allow it.
No doubt it is this, not the reflex
To hide something, which makes the hand loom large
As it retreats slightly. There is no way
To build it flat like a section of wall:
It must join the segment of a circle,

Roving back to the body of which it seems
So unlikely a part, to fence in and shore up the face
On which the effort of this condition reads
Like a pinpoint of a smile, a spark
Or star one is not sure of having seen
As darkness resumes. A perverse light whose
Imperative of subtlety dooms in advance its
Conceit to light up: unimportant but meant.
Francesco, your hand is big enough
To wreck the sphere, and too big,
One would think, to weave delicate meshes
That only argue its further detention.
(Big, but not coarse, merely on another scale,
Like a dozing whale on the sea bottom
In relation to the tiny, self-important ship
On the surface.) But your eyes proclaim
That everything is surface. The surface is what's there
And nothing can exist except what's there.
There are no recesses in the room, only alcoves,
And the window doesn't matter much, or that
Sliver of window or mirror on the right, even
As a gauge of the weather, which in French is
Le temps, the word for time, and which
Follows a course wherein changes are merely
Features of the whole. The whole is stable within
Instability, a globe like ours, resting
On a pedestal of vacuum, a ping-pong ball
Secure on its jet of water.
And just as there are no words for the surface, that is,
No words to say what it really is, that it is not
Superficial but a visible core, then there is
No way out of the problem of pathos vs. experience.

You will stay on, restive, serene in
Your gesture which is neither embrace nor warning
But which holds something of both in pure
Affirmation that doesn't affirm anything.

The balloon pops, the attention
Turns dully away. Clouds
In the puddle stir up into sawtoothed fragments.
I think of the friends
Who came to see me, of what yesterday
Was like. A peculiar slant
Of memory that intrudes on the dreaming model
In the silence of the studio as he considers
Lifting the pencil to the self-portrait.
How many people came and stayed a certain time,
Uttered light or dark speech that became part of you
Like light behind windblown fog and sand,
Filtered and influenced by it, until no part
Remains that is surely you. Those voices in the dusk
Have told you all and still the tale goes on
In the form of memories deposited in irregular
Clumps of crystals. Whose curved hand controls,
Francesco, the turning seasons and the thoughts
That peel off and fly away at breathless speeds
Like the last stubborn leaves ripped
From wet branches? I see in this only the chaos
Of your round mirror which organizes everything
Around the polestar of your eyes which are empty,
Know nothing, dream but reveal nothing.
I feel the carousel starting slowly
And going faster and faster: desk, papers, books,
Photographs of friends, the window and the trees

Merging in one neutral band that surrounds
Me on all sides, everywhere I look.
And I cannot explain the action of leveling,
Why it should all boil down to one
Uniform substance, a magma of interiors.
My guide in these matters is your self,
Firm, oblique, accepting everything with the same
Wraith of a smile, and as time speeds up so that it is soon
Much later, I can know only the straight way out,
The distance between us. Long ago
The strewn evidence meant something,
The small accidents and pleasures
Of the day as it moved gracelessly on,
A housewife doing chores. Impossible now
To restore those properties in the silver blur that is
The record of what you accomplished by sitting down
"With great art to copy all that you saw in the glass"
So as to perfect and rule out the extraneous
Forever. In the circle of your intentions certain spars
Remain that perpetuate the enchantment of self with self:
Eyebeams, muslin, coral. It doesn't matter
Because these are things as they are today
Before one's shadow ever grew
Out of the field into thoughts of tomorrow.

Tomorrow is easy, but today is uncharted,
Desolate, reluctant as any landscape
To yield what are laws of perspective
After all only to the painter's deep
Mistrust, a weak instrument though
Necessary. Of course some things

Are possible, it knows, but it doesn't know
Which ones. Some day we will try
To do as many things as are possible
And perhaps we shall succeed at a handful
Of them, but this will not have anything
To do with what is promised today, our
Landscape sweeping out from us to disappear
On the horizon. Today enough of a cover burnishes
To keep the supposition of promises together
In one piece of surface, letting one ramble
Back home from them so that these
Even stronger possibilities can remain
Whole without being tested. Actually
The skin of the bubble-chamber's as tough as
Reptile eggs; everything gets "programmed" there
In due course: more keeps getting included
Without adding to the sum, and just as one
Gets accustomed to a noise that
Kept one awake but now no longer does,
So the room contains this flow like an hourglass
Without varying in climate or quality
(Except perhaps to brighten bleakly and almost
Invisibly, in a focus of sharpening toward death—more
Of this later). What should be the vacuum of a dream
Becomes continually replete as the source of dreams
Is being tapped so that this one dream
May wax, flourish like a cabbage rose,
Defying sumptuary laws, leaving us
To awake and try to begin living in what
Has now become a slum. Sydney Freedberg in his
Parmigianino says of it: "Realism in this portrait

No longer produces an objective truth, but a *bizarria*. . . .
However its distortion does not create
A feeling of disharmony. . . . The forms retain
A strong measure of ideal beauty," because
Fed by our dreams, so inconsequential until one day
We notice the hole they left. Now their importance
If not their meaning is plain. They were to nourish
A dream which includes them all, as they are
Finally reversed in the accumulating mirror.
They seemed strange because we couldn't actually see
    them.
And we realize this only at a point where they lapse
Like a wave breaking on a rock, giving up
Its shape in a gesture which expresses that shape.
The forms retain a strong measure of ideal beauty
As they forage in secret on our idea of distortion.
Why be unhappy with this arrangement, since
Dreams prolong us as they are absorbed?
Something like living occurs, a movement
Out of the dream into its codification.

As I start to forget it
It presents its stereotype again
But it is an unfamiliar stereotype, the face
Riding at anchor, issued from hazards, soon
To accost others, "rather angel than man" (Vasari).
Perhaps an angel looks like everything
We have forgotten, I mean forgotten
Things that don't seem familiar when
We meet them again, lost beyond telling
Which were ours once. This would be the point

Of invading the privacy of this man who
"Dabbled in alchemy, but whose wish
Here was not to examine the subtleties of art
In a detached, scientific spirit: he wished through them
To impart the sense of novelty and amazement to the
    spectator"
(Freedberg). Later portraits such as the Uffizi
"Gentleman," the Borghese "Young Prelate" and
The Naples "Antea" issue from Mannerist
Tensions, but here, as Freedberg points out,
The surprise, the tension are in the concept
Rather than its realization.
The consonance of the High Renaissance
Is present, though distorted by the mirror.
What is novel is the extreme care in rendering
The velleities of the rounded reflecting surface
(It is the first mirror portrait),
So that you could be fooled for a moment
Before you realize the reflection
Isn't yours. You feel then like one of those
Hoffmann characters who have been deprived
Of a reflection, except that the whole of me
Is seen to be supplanted by the strict
Otherness of the painter in his
Other room. We have surprised him
At work, but no, he has surprised us
As he works. The picture is almost finished,
The surprise almost over, as when one looks out,
Startled by a snowfall which even now is
Ending in specks and sparkles of snow.
It happened while you were inside, asleep,

And there is no reason why you should have
Been awake for it, except that the day
Is ending and it will be hard for you
To get to sleep tonight, at least until late.

The shadow of the city injects its own
Urgency: Rome where Francesco
Was at work during the Sack: his inventions
Amazed the soldiers who burst in on him;
They decided to spare his life, but he left soon after;
Vienna where the painting is today, where
I saw it with Pierre in the summer of 1959; New York
Where I am now, which is a logarithm
Of other cities. Our landscape
Is alive with filiations, shuttlings;
Business is carried on by look, gesture,
Hearsay. It is another life to the city,
The backing of the looking glass of the
Unidentified but precisely sketched studio. It wants
To siphon off the life of the studio, deflate
Its mapped space to enactments, island it.
That operation has been temporarily stalled
But something new is on the way, a new preciosity
In the wind. Can you stand it,
Francesco? Are you strong enough for it?
This wind brings what it knows not, is
Self-propelled, blind, has no notion
Of itself. It is inertia that once
Acknowledged saps all activity, secret or public:
Whispers of the word that can't be understood
But can be felt, a chill, a blight

Moving outward along the capes and peninsulas
Of your nervures and so to the archipelagoes
And to the bathed, aired secrecy of the open sea.
This is its negative side. Its positive side is
Making you notice life and the stresses
That only seemed to go away, but now,
As this new mode questions, are seen to be
Hastening out of style. If they are to become classics
They must decide which side they are on.
Their reticence has undermined
The urban scenery, made its ambiguities
Look willful and tired, the games of an old man.
What we need now is this unlikely
Challenger pounding on the gates of an amazed
Castle. Your argument, Francesco,
Had begun to grow stale as no answer
Or answers were forthcoming. If it dissolves now
Into dust, that only means its time had come
Some time ago, but look now, and listen:
It may be that another life is stocked there
In recesses no one knew of; that it,
Not we, are the change; that we are in fact it
If we could get back to it, relive some of the way
It looked, turn our faces to the globe as it sets
And still be coming out all right:
Nerves normal, breath normal. Since it is a metaphor
Made to include us, we are a part of it and
Can live in it as in fact we have done,
Only leaving our minds bare for questioning
We now see will not take place at random
But in an orderly way that means to menace

Nobody—the normal way things are done,
Like the concentric growing up of days
Around a life: correctly, if you think about it.

A breeze like the turning of a page
Brings back your face: the moment
Takes such a big bite out of the haze
Of pleasant intuition it comes after.
The locking into place is "death itself,"
As Berg said of a phrase in Mahler's Ninth;
Or, to quote Imogen in *Cymbeline,* "There cannot
Be a pinch in death more sharp than this," for,
Though only exercise or tactic, it carries
The momentum of a conviction that had been building.
Mere forgetfulness cannot remove it
Nor wishing bring it back, as long as it remains
The white precipitate of its dream
In the climate of sighs flung across our world,
A cloth over a birdcage. But it is certain that
What is beautiful seems so only in relation to a specific
Life, experienced or not, channeled into some form
Steeped in the nostalgia of a collective past.
The light sinks today with an enthusiasm
I have known elsewhere, and known why
It seemed meaningful, that others felt this way
Years ago. I go on consulting
This mirror that is no longer mine
For as much brisk vacancy as is to be
My portion this time. And the vase is always full
Because there is only just so much room
And it accommodates everything. The sample
One sees is not to be taken as

Merely that, but as everything as it
May be imagined outside time—not as a gesture
But as all, in the refined, assimilable state.
But what is this universe the porch of
As it veers in and out, back and forth,
Refusing to surround us and still the only
Thing we can see? Love once
Tipped the scales but now is shadowed, invisible,
Though mysteriously present, around somewhere.
But we know it cannot be sandwiched
Between two adjacent moments, that its windings
Lead nowhere except to further tributaries
And that these empty themselves into a vague
Sense of something that can never be known
Even though it seems likely that each of us
Knows what it is and is capable of
Communicating it to the other. But the look
Some wear as a sign makes one want to
Push forward ignoring the apparent
Naïveté of the attempt, not caring
That no one is listening, since the light
Has been lit once and for all in their eyes
And is present, unimpaired, a permanent anomaly,
Awake and silent. On the surface of it
There seems no special reason why that light
Should be focused by love, or why
The city falling with its beautiful suburbs
Into space always less clear, less defined,
Should read as the support of its progress,
The easel upon which the drama unfolded
To its own satisfaction and to the end
Of our dreaming, as we had never imagined

It would end, in worn daylight with the painted
Promise showing through as a gage, a bond.
This nondescript, never-to-be defined daytime is
The secret of where it takes place
And we can no longer return to the various
Conflicting statements gathered, lapses of memory
Of the principal witnesses. All we know
Is that we are a little early, that
Today has that special, lapidary
Todayness that the sunlight reproduces
Faithfully in casting twig-shadows on blithe
Sidewalks. No previous day would have been like this.
I used to think they were all alike,
That the present always looked the same to everybody
But this confusion drains away as one
Is always cresting into one's present.
Yet the "poetic," straw-colored space
Of the long corridor that leads back to the painting,
Its darkening opposite—is this
Some figment of "art," not to be imagined
As real, let alone special? Hasn't it too its lair
In the present we are always escaping from
And falling back into, as the waterwheel of days
Pursues its uneventful, even serene course?
I think it is trying to say it is today
And we must get out of it even as the public
Is pushing through the museum now so as to
Be out by closing time. You can't live there.
The gray glaze of the past attacks all know-how:
Secrets of wash and finish that took a lifetime
To learn and are reduced to the status of
Black-and-white illustrations in a book where colorplates

Are rare. That is, all time
Reduces to no special time. No one
Alludes to the change; to do so might
Involve calling attention to oneself
Which would augment the dread of not getting out
Before having seen the whole collection
(Except for the sculptures in the basement:
They are where they belong).
Our time gets to be veiled, compromised
By the portrait's will to endure. It hints at
Our own, which we were hoping to keep hidden.
We don't need paintings or
Doggerel written by mature poets when
The explosion is so precise, so fine.
Is there any point even in acknowledging
The existence of all that? Does it
Exist? Certainly the leisure to
Indulge stately pastimes doesn't,
Any more. Today has no margins, the event arrives
Flush with its edges, is of the same substance,
Indistinguishable. "Play" is something else;
It exists, in a society specifically
Organized as a demonstration of itself.
There is no other way, and those assholes
Who would confuse everything with their mirror games
Which seem to multiply stakes and possibilities, or
At least confuse issues by means of an investing
Aura that would corrode the architecture
Of the whole in a haze of suppressed mockery,
Are beside the point. They are out of the game,
Which doesn't exist until they are out of it.
It seems like a very hostile universe

But as the principle of each individual thing is
Hostile to, exists at the expense of all the others
As philosophers have often pointed out, at least
This thing, the mute, undivided present,
Has the justification of logic, which
In this instance isn't a bad thing
Or wouldn't be, if the way of telling
Didn't somehow intrude, twisting the end result
Into a caricature of itself. This always
Happens, as in the game where
A whispered phrase passed around the room
Ends up as something completely different.
It is the principle that makes works of art so unlike
What the artist intended. Often he finds
He has omitted the thing he started out to say
In the first place. Seduced by flowers,
Explicit pleasures, he blames himself (though
Secretly satisfied with the result), imagining
He had a say in the matter and exercised
An option of which he was hardly conscious,
Unaware that necessity circumvents such resolutions
So as to create something new
For itself, that there is no other way,
That the history of creation proceeds according to
Stringent laws, and that things
Do get done in this way, but never the things
We set out to accomplish and wanted so desperately
To see come into being. Parmigianino
Must have realized this as he worked at his
Life-obstructing task. One is forced to read
The perfectly plausible accomplishment of a purpose
Into the smooth, perhaps even bland (but so

Enigmatic) finish. Is there anything
To be serious about beyond this otherness
That gets included in the most ordinary
Forms of daily activity, changing everything
Slightly and profoundly, and tearing the matter
Of creation, any creation, not just artistic creation
Out of our hands, to install it on some monstrous, near
Peak, too close to ignore, too far
For one to intervene? This otherness, this
"Not-being-us" is all there is to look at
In the mirror, though no one can say
How it came to be this way. A ship
Flying unknown colors has entered the harbor.
You are allowing extraneous matters
To break up your day, cloud the focus
Of the crystal ball. Its scene drifts away
Like vapor scattered on the wind. The fertile
Thought-associations that until now came
So easily, appear no more, or rarely. Their
Colorings are less intense, washed out
By autumn rains and winds, spoiled, muddied,
Given back to you because they are worthless.
Yet we are such creatures of habit that their
Implications are still around *en permanence,* confusing
Issues. To be serious only about sex
Is perhaps one way, but the sands are hissing
As they approach the beginning of the big slide
Into what happened. This past
Is now here: the painter's
Reflected face, in which we linger, receiving
Dreams and inspirations on an unassigned
Frequency, but the hues have turned metallic,

The curves and edges are not so rich. Each person
Has one big theory to explain the universe
But it doesn't tell the whole story
And in the end it is what is outside him
That matters, to him and especially to us
Who have been given no help whatever
In decoding our own man-size quotient and must rely
On second-hand knowledge. Yet I know
That no one else's taste is going to be
Any help, and might as well be ignored.
Once it seemed so perfect—gloss on the fine
Freckled skin, lips moistened as though about to part
Releasing speech, and the familiar look
Of clothes and furniture that one forgets.
This could have been our paradise: exotic
Refuge within an exhausted world, but that wasn't
In the cards, because it couldn't have been
The point. Aping naturalness may be the first step
Toward achieving an inner calm
But it is the first step only, and often
Remains a frozen gesture of welcome etched
On the air materializing behind it,
A convention. And we have really
No time for these, except to use them
For kindling. The sooner they are burnt up
The better for the roles we have to play.
Therefore I beseech you, withdraw that hand,
Offer it no longer as shield or greeting,
The shield of a greeting, Francesco:
There is room for one bullet in the chamber:
Our looking through the wrong end
Of the telescope as you fall back at a speed

Faster than that of light to flatten ultimately
Among the features of the room, an invitation
Never mailed, the "it was all a dream"
Syndrome, though the "all" tells tersely
Enough how it wasn't. Its existence
Was real, though troubled, and the ache
Of this waking dream can never drown out
The diagram still sketched on the wind,
Chosen, meant for me and materialized
In the disguising radiance of my room.
We have seen the city; it is the gibbous
Mirrored eye of an insect. All things happen
On its balcony and are resumed within,
But the action is the cold, syrupy flow
Of a pageant. One feels too confined,
Sifting the April sunlight for clues,
In the mere stillness of the ease of its
Parameter. The hand holds no chalk
And each part of the whole falls off
And cannot know it knew, except
Here and there, in cold pockets
Of remembrance, whispers out of time.

1977

Pyrography

Out here on Cottage Grove it matters. The galloping
Wind balks at its shadow. The carriages
Are drawn forward under a sky of fumed oak.
This is America calling:
The mirroring of state to state,
Of voice to voice on the wires,
The force of colloquial greetings like golden
Pollen sinking on the afternoon breeze.
In service stairs the sweet corruption thrives;
The page of dusk turns like a creaking revolving stage in
　　Warren, Ohio.

If this is the way it is let's leave,
They agree, and soon the slow boxcar journey begins,
Gradually accelerating until the gyrating fans of suburbs
Enfolding the darkness of cities are remembered
Only as a recurring tic. And midway
We meet the disappointed, returning ones, without its
Being able to stop us in the headlong night
Toward the nothing of the coast. At Bolinas
The houses doze and seem to wonder why through the
Pacific haze, and the dreams alternately glow and grow dull.
Why be hanging on here? Like kites, circling,
Slipping on a ramp of air, but always circling?

But the variable cloudiness is pouring it on,
Flooding back to you like the meaning of a joke.
The land wasn't immediately appealing; we built it
Partly over with fake ruins, in the image of ourselves:
An arch that terminates in mid-keystone, a crumbling stone
　　pier
For laundresses, an open-air theater, never completed

And only partially designed. How are we to inhabit
This space from which the fourth wall is invariably missing,
As in a stage-set or dollhouse, except by staying as we are,
In lost profile, facing the stars, with dozens of as yet
Unrealized projects, and a strict sense
Of time running out, of evening presenting
The tactfully folded-over bill? And we fit
Rather too easily into it, become transparent,
Almost ghosts. One day
The birds and animals in the pasture have absorbed
The color, the density of the surroundings,
The leaves are alive, and too heavy with life.

A long period of adjustment followed.
In the cities at the turn of the century they knew about it
But were careful not to let on as the iceman and the
    milkman
Disappeared down the block and the postman shouted
His daily rounds. The children under the trees knew it
But all the fathers returning home
On streetcars after a satisfying day at the office undid it:
The climate was still floral and all the wallpaper
In a million homes all over the land conspired to hide it.
One day we thought of painted furniture, of how
It just slightly changes everything in the room
And in the yard outside, and how, if we were going
To be able to write the history of our time, starting with
    today,
It would be necessary to model all these unimportant details
So as to be able to include them; otherwise the narrative
Would have that flat, sandpapered look the sky gets
Out in the middle west toward the end of summer,

The look of wanting to back out before the argument
Has been resolved, and at the same time to save appearances
So that tomorrow will be pure. Therefore, since we have to
    do our business
In spite of things, why not make it in spite of everything?
That way, maybe the feeble lakes and swamps
Of the back country will get plugged into the circuit
And not just the major events but the whole incredible
Mass of everything happening simultaneously and pairing
    off,
Channeling itself into history, will unroll
As carefully and as casually as a conversation in the next
    room,
And the purity of today will invest us like a breeze,
Only be hard, spare, ironical: something one can
Tip one's hat to and still get some use out of.

The parade is turning into our street.
My stars, the burnished uniforms and prismatic
Features of this instant belong here. The land
Is pulling away from the magic, glittering coastal towns
To an aforementioned rendezvous with August and
    December.
The hunch is it will always be this way,
The look, the way things first scared you
In the night light, and later turned out to be,
Yet still capable, all the same, of a narrow fidelity
To what you and they wanted to become:
No sighs like Russian music, only a vast unravelling
Out toward the junctions and to the darkness beyond
To these bare fields, built at today's expense.

1977

Daffy Duck in Hollywood

Something strange is creeping across me.
La Celestina has only to warble the first few bars
Of "I Thought about You" or something mellow from
Amadigi di Gaula for everything—a mint-condition can
Of Rumford's Baking Powder, a celluloid earring, Speedy
Gonzales, the latest from Helen Topping Miller's fertile
Escritoire, a sheaf of suggestive pix on greige, deckle-edged
Stock—to come clattering through the rainbow trellis
Where Pistachio Avenue rams the 2300 block of Highland
Fling Terrace. He promised he'd get me out of this one,
That mean old cartoonist, but just look what he's
Done to me now! I scarce dare approach me mug's
    attenuated
Reflection in yon hubcap, so jaundiced, so *déconfit*
Are its lineaments—fun, no doubt, for some quack
    phrenologist's
Fern-clogged waiting room, but hardly what you'd call
Companionable. But everything is getting choked to the
    point of
Silence. Just now a magnetic storm hung in the swatch of
    sky
Over the Fudds' garage, reducing it—drastically—
To the aura of a plumbago-blue log cabin on
A Gadsden Purchase commemorative cover. Suddenly all is
Loathing. I don't want to go back inside any more. You
    meet
Enough vague people on this emerald traffic-island—no,
Not people, comings and goings, more: mutterings,
    splatterings,
The bizarrely but effectively equipped infantries of happy-
    go-nutty
Vegetal jacqueries, plumed, pointed at the little

White cardboard castle over the mill run. "Up
The lazy river, how happy we could be?"
How will it end? That geranium glow
Over Anaheim's had the riot act read to it by the
Etna-size firecracker that exploded last minute into
A *carte du Tendre* in whose lower right-hand corner
(Hard by the jock-itch sand-trap that skirts
The asparagus patch of algolagnic *nuits blanches*) Amadis
Is cozening the Princesse de Clèves into a midnight
     micturition spree
On the Tamigi with the Wallets (Walt, Blossom, and little
Skeezix) on a lamé barge "borrowed" from Ollie
Of the Movies' dread mistress of the robes. Wait!
I have an announcement! This wide, tepidly meandering,
Civilized Lethe (one can barely make out the maypoles
And *châlets de nécessité* on its sedgy shore) leads to Tophet,
     that
Landfill-haunted, not-so-residential resort from which
Some travellers return! This whole moment is the groin
Of a borborygmic giant who even now
Is rolling over on us in his sleep. Farewell bocages,
Tanneries, water-meadows. The allegory comes unsnarled
Too soon; a shower of pecky acajou harpoons is
About all there is to be noted between tornadoes. I have
Only my intermittent life in your thoughts to live
Which is like thinking in another language. Everything
Depends on whether somebody reminds you of me.
That this is a fabulation, and that those "other times"
Are in fact the silences of the soul, picked out in
Diamonds on stygian velvet, matters less than it should.
Prodigies of timing may be arranged to convince them

We live in one dimension, they in ours. While I
Abroad through all the coasts of dark destruction seek
Deliverance for us all, think in that language: its
Grammar, though tortured, offers pavilions
At each new parting of the ways. Pastel
Ambulances scoop up the quick and hie them to hospitals.
"It's all bits and pieces, spangles, patches, really; nothing
Stands alone. What happened to creative evolution?"
Sighed Aglavaine. Then to her Sélysette: "If his
Achievement is only to end up less boring than the others,
What's keeping us here? Why not leave at once?
I have to stay here while they sit in there,
Laugh, drink, have fine time. In my day
One lay under the tough green leaves,
Pretending not to notice how they bled into
The sky's aqua, the wafted-away no-color of regions
        supposed
Not to concern us. And so we too
Came where the others came: nights of physical endurance,
Or if, by day, our behavior was anarchically
Correct, at least by New Brutalism standards, all then
Grew taciturn by previous agreement. We were spirited
Away *en bateau,* under cover of fudge dark.
It's not the incomplete importunes, but the spookiness
Of the finished product. True, to ask less were folly, yet
If he is the result of himself, how much the better
For him we ought to be! And how little, finally,
We take this into account! Is the puckered garance satin
Of a case that once held a brace of dueling pistols our
Only acknowledging of that color? I like not this,
Methinks, yet this disappointing sequel to ourselves

4 3

Has been applauded in London and St. Petersburg.
    Somewhere
Ravens pray for us."
                        The storm finished brewing. And thus
She questioned all who came in at the great gate, but none
She found who ever heard of Amadis,
Nor of stern Aureng-Zebe, his first love. Some
There were to whom this mattered not a jot: since all
By definition is completeness (so
In utter darkness they reasoned), why not
Accept it as it pleases to reveal itself? As when
Low skyscrapers from lower-hanging clouds reveal
A turret there, an art-deco escarpment here, and last perhaps
The pattern that may carry the sense, but
Stays hidden in the mysteries of pagination.
Not what we see but how we see it matters; all's
Alike, the same, and we greet him who announces
The change as we would greet the change itself.
All life is but a figment; conversely, the tiny
Tome that slips from your hand is not perhaps the
Missing link in this invisible picnic whose leverage
Shrouds our sense of it. Therefore bivouac we
On this great, blond highway, unimpeded by
Veiled scruples, worn conundrums. Morning is
Impermanent. Grab sex things, swing up
Over the horizon like a boy
On a fishing expedition. No one really knows
Or cares whether this is the whole of which parts
Were vouchsafed—once—but to be ambling on's
The tradition more than the safekeeping of it. This mulch
    for
Play keeps them interested and busy while the big,

Vaguer stuff can decide what it wants—what maps, what
Model cities, how much waste space. Life, our
Life anyway, is between. We don't mind
Or notice any more that the sky *is* green, a parrot
One, but have our earnest where it chances on us,
Disingenuous, intrigued, inviting more,
Always invoking the echo, a summer's day.

1977

It seems to me that my poetry sometimes proceeds as though an argument were suddenly derailed and something that started out clearly suddenly becomes opaque. It's a kind of mimesis of how experience comes to me: as one is listening to someone else—a lecturer, for instance—who's making perfect sense but suddenly slides into something that eludes one. What I am probably trying to do is to illustrate opacity and how it can suddenly descend over us, rather than trying to be willfully obscure.

Wet Casements

When Edward Raban, coming along the passage,
walked into the open doorway, he saw that it
was raining. It was not raining much.
      KAFKA, *WEDDING PREPARATIONS*
      IN THE COUNTRY

The conception is interesting: to see, as though reflected
In streaming windowpanes, the look of others through
Their own eyes. A digest of their correct impressions of
Their self-analytical attitudes overlaid by your
Ghostly transparent face. You in falbalas
Of some distant but not too distant era, the cosmetics,
The shoes perfectly pointed, drifting (how long you
Have been drifting; how long I have too for that matter)
Like a bottle-imp toward a surface which can never be
    approached,
Never pierced through into the timeless energy of a
    present
Which would have its own opinions on these matters,
Are an epistemological snapshot of the processes
That first mentioned your name at some crowded
    cocktail
Party long ago, and someone (not the person addressed)
Overheard it and carried that name around in his wallet
For years as the wallet crumbled and bills slid in
And out of it. I want that information very much today,

Can't have it, and this makes me angry.
I shall use my anger to build a bridge like that
Of Avignon, on which people may dance for the feeling

Of dancing on a bridge. I shall at last see my complete face
Reflected not in the water but in the worn stone floor of
 my bridge.

I shall keep to myself.
I shall not repeat others' comments about me.

1977

Unfortunately, I'm not very good at "explaining" my work. I once tried to do this in a question-and-answer period with some students of my friend Richard Howard, after which he told me: "They wanted the key to your work, but you presented them with a new set of locks." That sums up for me my feelings on the subject of "unlocking" my poetry. I'm unable to do so because I feel that my poetry is the explanation. The explanation of what? Of my thought, whatever that is. As I see it, my thought is both poetry and the attempt to explain that poetry; the two cannot be disentangled. . . . For me, poetry has its beginning and ending outside thought. Thought is certainly involved in the process; indeed, there are times when my work seems to me to be merely a recording of my thought processes without regard to what they are thinking about.

And *Ut Pictura Poesis* Is Her Name

You can't say it that way any more.
Bothered about beauty you have to
Come out into the open, into a clearing,
And rest. Certainly whatever funny happens to you
Is OK. To demand more than this would be strange
Of you, you who have so many lovers,
People who look up to you and are willing
To do things for you, but you think
It's not right, that if they really knew you . . .
So much for self-analysis. Now,
About what to put in your poem-painting:
Flowers are always nice, particularly delphinium.
Names of boys you once knew and their sleds,
Skyrockets are good—do they still exist?
There are a lot of other things of the same quality
As those I've mentioned. Now one must
Find a few important words, and a lot of low-keyed,
Dull-sounding ones. She approached me
About buying her desk. Suddenly the street was
Bananas and the clangor of Japanese instruments.
Humdrum testaments were scattered around. His head
Locked into mine. We were a seesaw. Something
Ought to be written about how this affects
You when you write poetry:
The extreme austerity of an almost empty mind
Colliding with the lush, Rousseau-like foliage of its desire
    to communicate
Something between breaths, if only for the sake
Of others and their desire to understand you and desert you
For other centers of communication, so that understanding
May begin, and in doing so be undone.

1977

My Erotic Double

He says he doesn't feel like working today.
It's just as well. Here in the shade
Behind the house, protected from street noises,
One can go over all kinds of old feeling,
Throw some away, keep others.
                                    The wordplay
Between us gets very intense when there are
Fewer feelings around to confuse things.
Another go-round? No, but the last things
You always find to say are charming, and rescue me
Before the night does. We are afloat
On our dreams as on a barge made of ice,
Shot through with questions and fissures of starlight
That keep us awake, thinking about the dreams
As they are happening. Some occurrence. You said it.

I said it but I can hide it. But I choose not to.
Thank you. You are a very pleasant person.
Thank you. You are too.

1977

At North Farm

Somewhere someone is traveling furiously toward you,
At incredible speed, traveling day and night,
Through blizzards and desert heat, across torrents, through
   narrow passes.
But will he know where to find you,
Recognize you when he sees you,
Give you the thing he has for you?

Hardly anything grows here,
Yet the granaries are bursting with meal,
The sacks of meal piled to the rafters.
The streams run with sweetness, fattening fish;
Birds darken the sky. Is it enough
That the dish of milk is set out at night,
That we think of him sometimes,
Sometimes and always, with mixed feelings?

1984

More Pleasant Adventures

The first year was like icing.
Then the cake started to show through.
Which was fine, too, except you forget the direction you're
    taking
Suddenly you are interested in some new thing
And can't tell how you got here. Then there is confusion
Even out of happiness, like a smoke—
The words get heavy, some topple over, you break others.
And outlines disappear once again.

Heck, it's anybody's story,
A sentimental journey—"gonna take a sentimental journey,"
And we do, but you wake up under the table of a dream:
You are that dream, and it is the seventh layer of you.
We haven't moved an inch, and everything has changed.
We are somewhere near a tennis court at night.
We get lost in life, but life knows where we are.
We can always be found with our associates.
Haven't you always wanted to curl up like a dog and go to
    sleep like a dog?

In the rash of partings and dyings (the new twist),
There's also room for breaking out of living.
Whatever happens will be quite ingenious.
No acre but will resume being disputed now,
And paintings are one thing we never seem to run out of.

1984

Around the Rough and Rugged Rocks the Ragged Rascal Rudely Ran

I think a lot about it,
Think quite a lot about it—
The omnipresent possibility of being interrupted
While what I stand for is still almost a bare canvas:
A few traceries, that may be fibers, perhaps
Not even these but shadows, hallucinations. . . .

And it is well then to recall
That this track is the outer rim of a flat crust,
Dimensionless, except for its poor, parched surface,
The face one raises to God,
Not the rich dark composite
We keep to ourselves,
Carpentered together any old way,
Coffee from an old tin can, a belch of daylight,
People leaving the beach.
If I could write it
And also write about it—
The interruption—
Rudeness on the face of it, but who
Knows anything about our behavior?

Forget what it is you're coming out of,
Always into something like a landscape
Where no one has ever walked
Because they're too busy.
Excitedly you open your rhyming dictionary.
It has begun to snow.

1984

This Room

The room I entered was a dream of this room.
Surely all those feet on the sofa were mine.
The oval portrait
of a dog was me at an early age.
Something shimmers, something is hushed up.

We had macaroni for lunch every day
except Sunday, when a small quail was induced
to be served to us. Why do I tell you these things?
You are not even here.

2000

I think that any one of my poems might be considered
a snapshot of whatever is going on in my mind at the
time—first of all the desire to write a poem, after that
wondering if I've left the oven on or thinking about
where I must be in the next hour.

Memories of Imperialism

Dewey took Manila
and soon after invented the decimal system
that keeps libraries from collapsing even unto this day.
A lot of mothers immediately started naming their male
    offspring "Dewey,"
which made him queasy. He was already having second
    thoughts about imperialism.
In his dreams he saw library books with milky numbers
on their spines floating in Manila Bay.
Soon even words like "vanilla" or "mantilla" would cause
    him to vomit.
The sight of a manila envelope precipitated him
into his study, where all day, with the blinds drawn,
he would press fingers against temples, muttering "What
    have I done?"
all the while. Then, gradually, he began feeling a bit better.
The world hadn't ended. He'd go for walks in his old
    neighborhood,
marveling at the changes there, or at the lack of them. "If
    one is
to go down in history, it is better to do so for two things
rather than one," he would stammer, none too
    meaningfully.

One day his wife took him aside
in her boudoir, pulling the black lace mantilla from her head
and across her bare breasts until his head was entangled in it.
"Honey, what am I supposed to say?" "Say nothing, you big
    boob.
Just be glad you got away with it and are famous."
    "Speaking of

boobs . . ." "Now you're getting the idea. Go file those
   books
on those shelves over there. Come back only when you're
   finished."

To this day schoolchildren wonder about his latter career
as a happy pedant, always nice with children, thoughtful
toward their parents. He wore a gray ceramic suit
walking his dog, a "bouledogue," he would point out.
People would peer at him from behind shutters, watchfully,
hoping no new calamities would break out, or indeed
that nothing more would happen, ever, that history had
   ended.
Yet it hadn't, as the admiral himself
would have been the first to acknowledge.

2000

Asked in 1995 by an earnest Yale student "What
is your relationship to the English language?"
Ashbery paused and answered, "Actually I write
in the American language. The American language
includes the English language."

Redeemed Area

Do you know where you live? Probably.
Abner is getting too old to drive but won't admit it.
The other day he got in his car to go buy some cough drops
of a kind they don't make anymore. And the drugstore
has been incorporated into a mall about seven miles away
with only about half the stores rented. There are three
other malls within a four-mile area. All the houses
are owned by the same guy, who's been renting
them out to college students for years, so they are virtually
    uninhabitable.
A smell of vitriol and socks pervades the area
like an open sewer in a souk. Anyway the cough drops
(a new brand) tasted pretty good—like catnip
or an orange slice that has lain on a girl's behind.

That's the electrician calling now—
nobody else would call before 7 A.M. Now we'll have some
electricity in the place. I'll start by plugging in
the Christmas tree lights. They were what made the whole
    thing
go up in sparks the last time. Next, the light
by the dictionary stand, so I can look some words up.
Then probably the toaster. A nice slice

of toast would really hit the spot now. I'm afraid it's all over
between us, though. Make nice, like you really cared,
I'll change my chemise, and we can dance around the room
like demented dogs, eager for a handout or they don't
know what. Gradually, everything will return to normal, I
promise you that. There'll be things for you to write about
in your diary, a fur coat for me, a lavish shoe tree for that
    other.

Make that two slices. I can see you only through a vegetal
　　murk
not unlike coral, if it were semi-liquid, or a transparent
　　milkshake.
I have adjusted the lamp,
morning's at seven,
the tarnish has fallen from the metallic embroidery, the walls
　　have fallen,
the country's pulse is racing. Parents are weeping,
the schools have closed.

All the fuss has put me in a good mood,
O great sun.

2000

But how can I be in this bar and also be a recluse?
The colony of ants was marching toward me, stretching
far into the distance, where they were as small as ants.
Their leader held up a twig as big as a poplar.
It was obviously supposed to be for me.
But he couldn't say it, with a poplar in his mandibles.
Well, let's forget that scene and turn to one in Paris.
Ants are walking down the Champs-Elysées
in the snow, in twos and threes, conversing,
revealing a sociability one never supposed them as having.
The larger ones have almost reached the allegorical statues
of French cities (is it?) on the Place de la Concorde.
"You see, I told you he was going to bolt.
Now he just sits in his attic
ordering copious *plats* from a nearby restaurant
as though God had meant him to be quiet."
"While you are like a portrait of Mme de Staël by
    Overbeck,
that is to say a little serious and washed out.
Remember you can come to me anytime
with what is bothering you, just don't ask for money.
Day and night my home, my hearth are open to you,
you great big adorable one, you."

The bar was unexpectedly comfortable.
I thought about staying. There was an alarm clock on it.
Patrons were invited to guess the time (the clock was always
    wrong).
More cheerful citizenry crowded in, singing the
    Marseillaise,
congratulating each other for the wrong reasons, like the
    color

of their socks, and taking swigs from a communal jug.
"I just love it when he gets this way,
which happens in the middle of August, when summer is
    on its way
out, and autumn is still just a glint in its eye,
a chronicle of hoar-frost foretold."
"Yes and he was going to buy all the candy bars in the
    machine
but something happened, the walls caved in (who knew
the river had risen rapidly?) and one by one people were
    swept away
calling endearing things to each other, using pet names.
'Achilles, meet Angus'," Then it all happened so quickly I
guess I never knew where we were going, where the
    pavement
was taking us.

Things got real quiet in the oubliette.
I was still reading *Jean-Christophe.* I'll never finish the darn
    thing.
Now is the time for you to go out into the light
and congratulate whoever is left in our city. People who
    survived
the eclipse. But I was totally taken with you, always have
    been.
Light a candle in my wreath, I'll be yours forever and will
    kiss you.

2 0 0 0

The Underwriters

Sir Joshua Lipton drank this tea
and liked it well enough to start selling it
to a few buddies, from the deck of his yacht.

It spread around the world, became a global
kind of thing. Today everybody knows its story,
and we must be careful not to offend our sponsors,
to humor their slightest whims, no matter how insane
they may seem to us at the time. Like the time one of them
wanted all the infants in the burg aged five or under
to be brought before him, wearing rose-colored sashes,
in order that he might read the Book of Job to them all day.
There were, as you may imagine, many tears shed,
flowing and flopping about, but in the end the old geezer
(the sponsor, not Job) was satisfied, and sank into a sleep
        more delicate
than any the world had ever known. You see what it's like
        here—
it's a madhouse, Sir, and I am planning to flee the first time
an occasion presents himself, say as a bag of laundry,
or the cargo of a muffin truck. Meanwhile, the "sands"
of time, as they call them, are slipping by with scarcely a
        whisper
except for the most lynx-eyed among us. We'll make do,

another day, shopping and such, bringing the meat home at
        night
all roseate and gleaming, ready for the frying pan.
Our names will be read off a rollcall we won't hear—
how could we? We're not even born yet—the stars will
        perform their dance
privately, for us, and the pictures in the great black book

that opens at night will enchant us with their yellow
    harmonies.
We'll manage to get back, someday, to the tie siding where
    the idea
of all this began, frustrated and a little hungry, but eager
to hear each others' tales of what went on in the interim
of our long lives, what the tea leaves said
and whether it turned out that way. I'll brush your bangs
a little, you'll lean against my hip for comfort.

2000

Poets, as has often been noted, in writing about other
poets tend to write about themselves, even to the point
of seeing as faults in others what they take to be virtues
in themselves.

SUGGESTIONS FOR FURTHER READING:

Books by John Ashbery

The Mooring of Starting Out: The First Five Books of Poetry (Ecco Press, 1997)

Self-Portrait in a Convex Mirror (Penguin Books, 1992)

Three Books: Houseboat Days/Shadow Train/A Wave (Penguin Books, 1993)

Selected Poems (Viking, 1985)

Your Name Here (Farrar, Straus & Giroux, 2000)

Books about John Ashbery

On the Outside Looking Out, John Shoptaw (Harvard University Press, 1994)

Five Temperaments, David Kalstone (Oxford University Press, 1977)

Beyond Amazement: New Essays on John Ashbery, David Lehman, ed. (Cornell University Press, 1980)

The Last Avant-Garde: The Making of the New York School of Poets, David Lehman (Doubleday, 1998)

John Ashbery: Modern Critical Views, Harold Bloom, ed. (Chelsea House, 1985)

The Tribe of John: Ashbery and Contemporary Poetry, Susan Schultz, ed. (University of Alabama Press, 1997)

Acknowledgments

Special thanks for their most generous assistance and support to John Ashbery, David Kermani, Lourdes Lopez, Richard Warren, director of The Historical Sound Recordings Collection, Sterling Memorial Library, Yale University, and The Axe-Houghton Foundation.

Recordings of John Ashbery are included by permission of John Ashbery. "Soonest Mended," "Parergon," "Self-Portrait in a Convex Mirror," "Pyrography," "Daffy Duck in Hollywood," and "And *Ut Pictura Poesis* Is Her Name" are made available through the courtesy of the Department of English, Yale University. "Wet Casements," "My Erotic Double," "At North Farm," "More Pleasant Adventures," "Around The Rough and Rugged Rocks the Ragged Rascal Rudely Ran," "This Room," "Memories of Imperialism," "Redeemed Area," "Your Name Here," and "The Underwriters" were recorded in Carnegie Hall Recording Studios, New York City, October, 2000, and are made available by permission of the author.

Cover photograph: Don Haberman. Interior photographs and ms. page courtesy of John Ashbery.

A Designs for Learning Production
Series Producer: Jane Garmey
Series Designer: Chip Kidd